For Mrs. Hewett,
my kindergarten teacher.
Thank you for instilling in me
a love of storytelling.

There once was a lady
who lived in an

ORDINARY

house with two
ordinary cats who were fed by an
ordinary man with an
extraordinary beard.

The lady was going to have a baby!
Everyone was happy for the lady and the man with
the beard, but the lady was happy AND scared.
She did not like change. She liked her
life as it was...

ORDINARY.

One day, the lady came home and noticed something was different. There was a bright orange, bushy-tailed cat asleep on the couch!

"Well," said the lady, "you are NOT my cat!"

And the other cats AGREED.

The lady put the cat outside. Before she could blink, the cat came back in!

She put the silly orange cat out once more and said "you are NOT my cat!"

The cat DISAGREED.

When the lady woke up the next morning,
the silly orange cat was sitting on her nightstand.

Not My Cat wanted to play!

Not My Cat loved to play,
and the more she played,
the more the lady laughed.

Not My Cat had a favorite game. It was called

"WHAT IS THAT UNDER THE SHEETS?!"

Over the next few weeks, Not My Cat
became a good helper.

She helped brush the lady's teeth...

dusted the blinds...

and occupied the sink so it wouldn't feel so drained.

At Christmas time, she helped the lady decorate the tree,

and wrap the presents.

As time passed, the lady's baby grew inside her, and she began to realize that Not My Cat was anything BUT ordinary. Not My Cat helped put the crib together and put the baby items away.

The lady began to love all things extraordinary!
She was not scared anymore,
and soon she realized she was ready for the baby.

The lady had her baby and brought her home. Not My Cat watched the baby to make sure she was safe. Not My Cat knew how scary this world must be for something so small and

...hairless.

Not My Cat tested out the baby's toys and bathmat. She went on walks with the baby and the lady, and when she got tired, she would ride in the stroller, too.

She sometimes wondered why the baby
MEOWED
so loud.

When it was time for the baby to try food, Not My Cat tested it to make sure it was good.

It was not.

Not My Cat decided this baby was adjusting well.

Her job was done.

Not My Cat left just as quickly as she had come.

The lady was very sad. She missed her extraordinary cat, but she was happy that Not My Cat showed her that

life was never ordinary.

As it turned out, the baby grew into an
extraordinary little girl!
The lady still missed Not My Cat, but life was moving quickly.
She knew Not My Cat was helping another family now.

One day, the lady surprised the
little girl with a kitten.
Not just any kitten...an orange kitten!

"My cat!" shouted the girl.

And he was her cat.
Her perfect, extraordinary,
orange cat.

CPSIA information can be obtained
at www.ICGtesting.com
Printed in the USA
BVRC090822191021
619179BV00021B/424